Granny Rainbow

Katherine Hetzel

Panda Eyes

Published in 2014 by Panda Eyes Publishers Ltd,
Loughborough, Leicestershire.

ISBN 978 0 9571027 4 3

A CIP catalogue record for this title is available from
the British Library.

Printed and bound by Design and Print Services,
Loughborough University.

Cover design by Imran Siddiq.

*For Copper Bottom, Jenny B
and T Bob, with love x*

Granny Rainbow...

Acknowledgements

How Granny Rainbow happened...

10 fun facts about Katherine

10 fun facts about Laura

Granny Rainbow and the Black Shadow

It all started with the roses in Old Tom's garden.

He loved *all* the flowers he grew, but the roses were his pride and joy; their bright yellow petals cheered him up on even the rainiest day. Well, they used to – until the morning he went into the garden and his roses weren't sunshine yellow any more.

They were grey.

Tom scratched his head; he'd never seen anything like it. He shuffled into the shed, mixed up some of his special organic growing juice, and watered the bushes.

It made no difference; the colour didn't come back.

Then Marta Tarter's curtains – the green and blue striped ones – lost their colour too.

'It's awful!' she wailed to Old Tom. 'Who on earth has grey-striped curtains hanging at their windows?'

'Well…you do, now,' he said, which wasn't very helpful.

It didn't stop there. Over the next week, colour

disappeared from all over the village – from little Timmy Tenta's orange scarf, Mother Harberd's strawberry jam, Colonel Green's medal ribbons and a whole host of other things besides. It was as though a colour thief crept through the village each evening and nothing was safe from his or her attention.

The once colourful community became a drab shadow of its former self, the villagers wearing frowns and solemn expressions instead of their usual happy smiles.

'This won't do!' Old Tom said, gnashing his false teeth so hard they fell out. 'I'm away to see Granny Rainbow,' he announced, once he'd put them back in.

*

The path to Granny Rainbow's cottage wound out of the village and up the hill behind it. Old Tom leaned heavily on his walking stick as he climbed higher, pausing now and again for a rest. Once, he looked down at the village nestling in the valley; from here, he could see many grey patches. The lack of colour was like a disease, spreading across the familiar landscape.

'At least there's no grey up here yet,' Tom

muttered to a red-chested robin who was peering at him with bright eyes. The robin sang a few notes in reply and flew off in the direction Tom knew he needed to go. So he straightened his shoulders and set off after it. Eventually he rounded a bend and there was Granny Rainbow's cottage in front of him, nestled in a hollow beside the path.

No-one, not even Old Tom, could remember Granny Rainbow's real name, but everyone knew why she was called Granny Rainbow. Her garden was a riot of colour; it was as though a painter with a new paint-box had run wild, dabbing everything in sight with whatever shade had taken his fancy. The borders were crammed with an untidy mess of flowers that reminded Tom of the inside of a kaleidoscope, and the lawn was a brighter green than he thought it had any right to be.

The cottage's bright blue front door hung wide open and there, standing in the doorway with her green eyes twinkling merrily over half moon spectacles, was Granny Rainbow herself.

'Well!' she laughed. 'It's not often I have a visitor. Come on in, Tom. I'll put the kettle on.'

With a sigh of relief, Old Tom sank onto a
bench underneath a pink cherry-blossom tree and gazed
around the garden. Fat black-and-yellow bees buzzed
around the lavender, drunk on nectar. Brown- and red-
feathered chickens scratched happily under the hedge.

A marmalade cat lay asleep in a patch of sun and tiny purple and yellow butterflies flitted round his head as though they were dancing to music only they could hear. Tom realised just how much he'd missed seeing colour in the village.

'Here you go.' Granny set a tray down on a tree stump. 'One lump or two?' she asked, handing Old Tom a mug brimming with fragrant tea.

'Three please,' Tom said, and helped himself to a slice of cherry cake as three sugar lumps plopped into his mug. Only when the last bite of cake had vanished and the last few crumbs had been brushed onto the floor for the chickens, did Granny Rainbow break the silence.

'So. What brings you to my cottage, old friend?'

Tom sighed. 'Granny, we need your help. We're losing all our colour.'

Granny Rainbow listened patiently while Tom explained, even when he got out his notebook and read through the very long list of everything that had been affected by greyness.

'Hmm,' she said when he'd finished. 'It's an unusual case, but I think I can help. Come into my workroom. I'll see what I can do.'

Her workroom was just inside the front door. It was a small room, brightly lit and lined with hundreds of narrow shelves. The shelves were filled with bottles...and the bottles were crammed with coloured powders. Old Tom stared in amazement and tried to name them all in his head...turquoise, cerise, vermillion, citrine, ochre, sapphire, ruby, lime, primrose, russet...In the end, he ran out of words to describe them all – he couldn't believe so many colours even existed!

Granny consulted Tom's list before peering at the shelves. She selected several bottles and carefully weighed their powders out on a tiny set of brass scales. Then she chose a few more. Sometimes she paused, checking with Tom that she'd chosen just the right shade. He couldn't always remember the colour exactly, so he would just nod, hoping he was right.

Finally, Granny Rainbow added the last powder, a particularly pale blue that Old Tom knew had coloured Marta Tarter's best china tea-cups, and gave the mixture a good stir. 'Here you go,' she said, handing over a tightly stoppered bottle.

Tom looked at it dubiously.

12

'At midnight tonight, under the full moon,' Granny told him, 'sprinkle this powder along the length of Main Street. Come the morning, everything should be restored to its rightful colour. Or as close as we can remember,' she added with a smile.

'Thank 'ee kindly, Granny.' A flash of vivid yellow in the mixture caught Tom's eye. 'I'll be glad to get my sunshine roses back.'

At midnight, with the man in the moon looking on, Old Tom did just as Granny Rainbow had ordered; shuffled through the village, sprinkling the precious powder along the road.

The next morning, what a sight! The colour was back – even in Marta Tarter's tea-cups. Old Tom spent a happy morning tending his roses and listening to the delighted cries of his neighbours as they discovered yet another item that had been un-greyed. Music played, the children danced and sang, and all seemed well with the world.

But just before lunchtime, a dark cloud seemed to roll across the sun, and Tom looked up from his roses, startled.

Coming up the road was a man, dressed all in

black. He carried an ebony cane, topped with a large lump of dark stone. Long strides soon brought him level with Old Tom, and there the man halted, his dark gaze sweeping over the garden.

'Hullo,' Old Tom said. It never hurt to be polite.

'It sounds like there's something to celebrate in the village,' said the man.

'There is. The return of colour!' Tom's arm swept out as though embracing his flowers.

'You have plenty of it now,' the stranger murmured, his eyes darting towards the yellow rose bush. 'Yet I believe that yesterday, there was a lot less?'

A shiver of unease rippled down Tom's spine. How did the stranger know that? 'That's as may be,' he said. 'But what business is it of yours?'

The stranger's eyes narrowed. Because I…am the Black Shadow,' he whispered, and raised his cane.

Old Tom stared at the black stone and suddenly understood what he could see swirling at its heart.

'You're the colour thief!' he gasped. 'Why would you do that?'

'Why?' The Black Shadow scowled. 'What is

14

the point of wasting colour on the world? All it does is make people happy, and I don't like happiness.' The dark eyes rested on the old man. 'I had taken many colours from this place and left it most miserable. I want to know how you replaced it all, so that the next time I leave things grey, they stay that way.'

Tom tried very hard to look brave, but his insides were all of a quiver when he felt those eyes boring into him. 'Not telling!' he snapped.

'Is that so?' Pushing open the gate and forcing Old Tom aside, the Shadow walked uninvited into the garden. 'What about if I do…this?' The black stone touched a clump of forget-me-nots growing beside the path.

Right in front of Tom's unbelieving eyes, the colour bled right out of them. A spark of blue flashed in the stone and disappeared. 'Still not telling,' he growled.

A slow, wicked smile spread across the Black Shadow's face. 'Oh, you'll tell, old man. You'll tell. Watch…' He walked further along the path, touching carnations and lilies and daisies and clematis and lavender with the end of his cane. Each time, their colour was sucked into the stone and disappeared. But it was pointless. Old Tom stubbornly refused to reveal the secret. Until, that is, the moment when the Black Shadow stood beside the only colourful thing left in the garden.

A bush filled with sunshine yellow roses.

'Sure you won't tell?' the Black Shadow purred, and a single bud of Tom's pride and joy turned the colour of granite when the black stone kissed it.

Tom's heart sank. He really, really didn't want to lose his sunshine roses again. Should he tell the Black Shadow about Granny Rainbow? She had more than enough colour in her garden, after all. Surely she could spare some of it for the Black Shadow so that Tom could at least keep his roses safe? Trying to convince himself that Granny Rainbow wouldn't mind, not really – she'd do anything to help, he was sure – Old Tom made up his mind.

'You need to speak to Granny Rainbow,' he blurted out, one eye on the cane still hovering dangerously close to the next rosebud.

'Granny Rainbow?'

Old Tom nodded quickly. 'Granny Rainbow. Follow the path up the hill. You can't miss her.'

Without another word, the Black Shadow turned on his heel and strode away.

'Oh dear,' said Tom, and shuffled as quickly as he could into his house, locking the door behind him.

*

At teatime, Old Tom had a visitor.

'Coo-ee!' Granny Rainbow called through the letterbox.

Old Tom hid behind the settee. He didn't want to see Granny at all – not if the Black Shadow had, like he feared, taken all her colours.

'Tom! I know you're in there! Open up!'

He peered around the edge of the settee and saw a pair of green eyes peering back at him through the rectangular slot that was more used to having letters pushed through it.

'I've got something for you,' Granny called.

'So long as it's not a big stick to beat me with,' Old Tom muttered, but curiosity had got the better of him. He shuffled to the door, pulled back the bolts and opened it a crack. 'What have you got?'

Granny beamed. 'Your colours. Do you want them back?'

'What? But - the Black Shadow! How? When? Yes! Yes please!' Tom flung the door open, ready to give Granny an enormous squeeze. He froze when he saw what she held in her hand. 'The Black Shadow's cane!' he gasped. For one second, he thought maybe

Granny Rainbow was going to use it on him – but her merry smile and the crinkles at the corners of her eyes soon reassured him.

'Yes,' she said, twirling the cane rather cleverly round her head. 'He left it behind.'

'Eh?' Old Tom scratched his head. 'Why'd he do that?'

'Well…' Granny Rainbow avoided Tom's eye. 'I…told him a less tiresome way he could capture colour instead.'

'You what?' Old Tom almost exploded from indignation, but then he caught sight of Granny's face. There was something there – a sparkle in her eye and just a hint of mischief around her mouth. 'How's he going to manage that then, without his stick?' he asked suspiciously.

'I told him that if he could catch the end of a rainbow and roll it up, then there'd be no colour in the world, ever again. Everything would be black and white. He seemed quite captivated by the idea.'

'But everyone knows, you can't catch…' A deep chuckle began somewhere in Old Tom's boots and worked its way upwards until it burst from his lips.

'That's really rather clever of you.'

Granny threw back her head and laughed. 'Too true, my friend. There'll be no more greyness in this village or anywhere else for that matter. Which reminds me – let's liven things up in your garden, shall we?'

Five minutes, a pair of pliers and a lot of puffing later, the stone finally came free from the end of the Black Shadow's cane. Granny Rainbow, using Old Tom's favourite sugar tongs, carefully placed it on a large rock in the middle of the garden.

'Thrush usually bashes snails on that,' Tom said.

'Mr Thrush will have to wait. We're going to do some bashing of our own in a minute,' Granny Rainbow said. 'Got the hammer? Right. Hit it. Just there.'

Tom brought his sledgehammer down hard and the black stone shattered into a million pieces.

Old Tom and Granny both ducked as coloured sparks shot out of its heart and whizzed over their heads, zooming and zigzagging in every direction. When they landed on the flower from which they'd been taken, the sparks fizzed for a moment and then disappeared with a pop. Once again the lilies were orange, the carnations pink, the clematis were re-striped purple and pink, and the daisies got their yellow middles back. As for the granite coloured rosebud…its tiny yellow spark was the last to arrive. Old Tom watched contentedly as the bud returned to its normal colour.

In the distance, the sky grew dark and thunder rumbled, yet over the village it remained bright and sunny.

'Looks like we might be in for a storm,' Old Tom observed. 'Wonder if there'll be a rainbow?' He cast a sideways glance at Granny, and wasn't surprised to see her grinning like a Cheshire cat. 'How long d'you think it'll be? Before the Black Shadow realises he's never going to catch one?'

'For ever, I hope,' laughed Granny Rainbow.

Granny Rainbow and the Purple Potion

It all started with a dreadful noise.

'What on earth's that racket?' Old Tom leapt up from his favourite armchair as fast as he could; it took him a little while. 'If it's Arnie Thunk, pulling Mrs Fluffy's tail again, I'll make him screech too!'

Tom grabbed the broom from the hall, ready to see Arnie off. Just as he opened the front door, Mrs Fluffy shot past him like a streak of furry lightning. She clawed her way to the top of the curtains and clung precariously to the curtain rail, hissing and spitting.

And still, the noise continued. It really was terrible – a set-your-false-teeth-on-edge kind of screech.

'Hmm,' said Old Tom, peering up at the black and white furball that was Mrs Fluffy. 'Well, if it isn't you making the noise, who is?' He gripped the broom a little tighter and stepped outside, following the dreadful sound right to the very end of his garden, where the broad beans grew. It had been a good year for broad beans and Tom was very proud of how well the plants were growing up their poles. But he realised now that it meant he couldn't see the cause of the deafening screeching and scraping which was *still* coming from behind them.

Very carefully, Tom peered round the beans.

'Well, bless my soul, it's little Timmy Tenta!'

The screeching stopped.

'Hullo, Mr Tom.'

Although relieved to find that no animals were being tortured, Old Tom was still puzzled by the presence of a ginger-headed lad, holding a violin in one hand and a bow in the other, at the end of his garden.

'So…it was you making that awful din, was it?'

Timmy's eyes filled. A large tear plopped onto the ground from the end of his nose and he murmured something that Tom couldn't quite catch.

'Eh? What's that you say?'

'I know I'm terrible,' Timmy sniffed. 'I'll never win the scooter…'

'Scooter? Here, use this. Not your sleeve.' Old Tom felt horribly guilty for upsetting the lad, and racked his brain to think of something to make amends while Timmy blew his nose rather loudly into the grubby handkerchief.

'I've got some lemonade in the kitchen,' Old

Tom said eventually, stuffing the soggy hankie back in his pocket. 'How's about you bring your fiddle and tell me all about this 'ere scooter and how they're connected?'

Back inside, Mrs Fluffy had climbed down from the curtains. Tom decided he'd better not tell Timmy where she'd been and why. Instead, he let the boy fuss the old moggy while he fetched a couple of glasses and filled them with cloudy lemonade.

'Sit down lad, and drink this.' Old Tom slurped his lemonade just as loudly as Timmy. 'Ah! That's better. Now...' He leaned back in his chair and fixed Timmy with a beady eye. 'What's all this about a scooter and a fiddle?'

'Violin.' Timmy blinked at him. 'It's for the talent contest. Miss Percival is holding it in three weeks time at the end of term, and everyone is supposed to do something. Jane's doing a dance, Billy's juggling, Ted's singing, Myra's playing the flute and - '

'I understand,' interrupted Tom, keen not to hear what everyone in the class was going to do.

'They're all so much better than me. I've tried to practice, but I seem to be getting worse. Mum sent me to the bottom of our garden 'cos I kept waking the baby. She said she could still hear me and I had to go further away. I'm never going to be good enough to win the scooter and I really, really want to win it.'

'Ah…' Old Tom looked at Timmy's sad little face and thought about things for a moment or two. He guessed that since the new baby's arrival – number seven if he remembered right – money was a bit tight in the Tenta house. Timmy wouldn't be getting a scooter any time soon. Unless he won one.

Into Tom's head sprang the name of someone who might be able to help. 'How about you, me and the fiddle take a little walk?' he said.

*

When they got to Granny Rainbow's cottage, it was Old Tom who explained the problem; Timmy was too busy fussing her cat, Marmaduke.

'He can't be that bad,' Granny whispered.

'You reckon?' Old Tom smiled grimly and called to Timmy. 'Why don't you play your tune for Granny?'

Timmy picked up his discarded violin, sighed a huge sigh and tucked the instrument under his chin.

'What are you going to play?' Granny asked.

'In an English country garden.' With his tongue sticking out and his eyes glued to his fingers, Timmy drew the bow across the strings.

Granny Rainbow's smile looked awfully twisted by the time the tune was finished, but at least she managed to keep it in place. Marmaduke, like Mrs Fluffy, had voted with his feet.

'All the right notes, just none of 'em in the right order,' Tom muttered darkly.

'I'm useless,' Timmy wailed, and plonked himself down on the carpet.

'I wouldn't say that.' Granny shot a warning look at Old Tom when he harrumphed rather too loudly. 'I've been thinking…I have a special potion, which can be used for exactly this kind of situation. I wouldn't let just anyone have it, but I think in this case…'

She led Timmy into her workroom, where he stared, goggle-eyed, at the shelves. He'd never seen so many colours in one place, all stored separately in tiny little bottles. What on earth was Granny going to make for him?

'Right then…' Granny Rainbow lit a little oil burner and set a kettle over it. 'I'm going to make you some Purple Potion,' she told Timmy. She ran her finger slowly along the shelf of purple powders until the kettle began to whistle. At that point, the finger stopped beside a slightly larger jar, filled to the brim with pale violet crystals.

'Aha! This is the one.' Under Timmy's curious gaze, she took a good spoonful of the coarse powder and mixed it in some boiled water until the crystals dissolved and the water turned the same violet colour. Carefully she poured the liquid into an empty glass bottle and stoppered it with a cork.

'Now, this must be our secret,' Granny warned, holding out the bottle and its precious contents to Timmy. 'There's enough Purple Potion here to take three times a week. One spoonful, swallowed just before you play your violin. You'll be amazed at what happens.'

'Really? It'll make me play better?' Timmy's gaze flicked between the bottle and Granny's smiling face.

'Oh, yes. And I'm sure Tom won't mind you continuing to practise behind his beans, will you, Tom?'

Old Tom quickly changed his grimace to a smile when Timmy's hopeful face turned towards him.

'Really, Mr Tom? You won't mind if I make a noise?'

29

'Nope.' Old Tom paused. 'How long did you say it was to the show?'

*

For three more weeks, for an hour every Monday, Wednesday and Friday, Timmy Tenta practiced his violin behind Tom's beans. If it was sunny, he stayed outside to play – if it was wet, he played in the shed.

In the first week, Old Tom found he was often hoping for rain, because at least the shed walls deadened the sound a bit.

'Purple Potion don't seem to be helping much, does it?' he said to Mrs Fluffy, who had taken up residence on top of the curtain rail again.

In the second week, Tom could recognise a few bars and by the third week, found he could actually bear to be out in the garden while Timmy practiced, whistling along to the tune while he weeded the flower beds. Even Mrs Fluffy grew used to the violin – she crept closer to Timmy every day until eventually, she wound herself around his legs while he was playing.

The day of the contest finally arrived. Timmy Tenta had sent both Old Tom and Granny Rainbow an invitation, but as much as Tom tried to make his excuses – he'd rather cut his toenails than sit through an hour or so of talent show – Granny insisted that he had to go.

And so it was that Old Tom, wearing his best tie – the one with yellow roses on it – and a suit that smelled only faintly of mothballs, shuffled into the village hall beside a very excited Granny Rainbow.

'I can't wait!' she said, waving at several of the villagers. 'I'm keeping all my fingers and toes crossed for Timmy.'

Even as the words left her mouth, a distraught Timmy rushed over to them.

'Why, Timmy, whatever is wrong?' Granny said, drawing him away from the crowd of parents and well-wishers.

'What'll I do? There's none left – look!' Timmy held up the little glass bottle. Only a few drops of the Purple Potion remained.

'Hardly enough in there to even wet your whistle,' Tom grunted.

'Please, Granny Rainbow, please make some more! I can't play my violin without it – I can't!'

Granny smiled gently. 'Of course you can.'

31

'I can't! I tried just now and I can't play a note!' Fresh tears, huge and glistening, sprang into Timmy's eyes. 'I need the magic potion!'

'My dear Timmy.' Granny found a couple of empty seats at the back of the hall and sat Timmy down beside her. She took his trembling hand in her own and patted it. 'Old Tom was telling me just now how much you'd improved and that he thought you could play perfectly well without it. Didn't you, Tom?'

'Eh? Wassat?' Old Tom's brain finally caught up with Granny's words. 'Oh, aye…yes, much better. I can even recognise the tune now. Don't need any magic potion at all, not now. Fine without it. Even Mrs Fluffy thinks so.'

'Really?' Timmy's watery eyes blinked twice.

'Really.' Tom nodded.

A slight frown creased Granny Rainbow's brow. 'Some people might think it was unfair to use magic in the competition. It would be like cheating.'

Timmy thought for a moment or two. Then he straightened his shoulders and wiped his nose on his sleeve. 'You're right. I know I've got a little bit better. I'll just have to do the best I can.'

'Good lad. Off you go, then. I can see Miss Percival looking for you.'

*

Old Tom walked home with Granny after the show. They were almost at his gate when Timmy screeched to a halt beside them on his new scooter.

'Look, Granny! Look, Mr Tom! I wouldn't have got this without your Purple Potion. Thank you!' He did a couple of circuits round them, making Tom feel rather dizzy, before shooting off in the direction of home again.

Tom humphed. 'I'm hoping 'e'll find somewhere new to practice from now on. Amazing, what a bit of magic potion can do.'

Granny laughed. 'Not you too, Tom?'

Tom's brow furrowed. 'Eh? What d'you mean?'

'Well, that potion was no more magic than the water in your rain barrel.'

Tom scratched his head. 'B-but – he took the potion every time he came up for a practice! You heard him at the start - awful noise, awful! He couldn't have got as good as he did without a bit of magic.'

'Yes, he could.' Granny's eyes twinkled.

'There really wasn't anything special at all about the Purple Potion. The 'powder' I used was just coloured sugar. I usually sprinkle it on my fairy cakes. But taking a spoonful of something before he played was just enough to help build Timmy's confidence.'

'So you made it so he thought he *could* play?'

'He could,' Granny said. 'He just needed to believe it.'

'Ah.' Tom began to smile as he realised where the real magic had come from. 'And I suppose hours of practice behind the beans or in the shed do wonders for a budding violinist, don't they?'

Granny Rainbow nodded and grinned. 'They do, Tom. They certainly do.'

Granny Rainbow and the Blue-footed Twitterer

It all started with a twitcher.

Rodger Randoodle, to be precise. He lived in a cottage with a big garden and a little wood beyond. As such, it was ideally placed to allow him to enjoy his favourite past-time: birdwatching.

No-one – absolutely no-one – could match Rodger's knowledge of birds.

Any bird visiting Rodger's garden was spoilt for choice as to the menu. Mealworms wriggled in a deep tray, sunflower seeds and niger seeds and peanuts packed the decorative feeders dotted about the borders, and lard cake was squashed into the coconut shells which hung in the trees. The finches were able to strip the seeds from thistle heads and blackbirds hopped along the lawn, heads cocked sideways as they listened for the sound of worms wriggling under the lush grass. The wren and robin could fight over tiny bits of cheese and apple left specially on the bird table for them, and once fed, the great tits would perform acrobatics in the pear tree while the pigeons strutted around like they owned the place.

Rodger could tell a greater spotted woodpecker from a lesser spotted one, knew exactly where the robin liked to nest (in an old kettle under the holly bush) and kept the bushes thick for the sparrows to roost in. In fact, there was such a profusion of birds attracted to Rodger's garden that the dawn chorus was always deafening. His neighbours had taken to wearing ear muffs in bed.

But as much as he loved his birds, there was one thing that Rodger hated with an equal passion – and it was that which sent him marching off to Old Tom's cottage early one morning.

'Oh 'eck,' said Old Tom, as he watched Rodger bearing down on him.

'I want a word with you!'

'What's up?' Tom racked his brain to think of what he might have done to upset Rodger. He'd never seen the poor man in such a state; Rodger's face was the colour of beetroot, his eyes were flashing sparks, and his beard was positively bristling.

'Your cat! That's what's up!' Rodger shook his fist, narrowly missing Tom's nose.

'Mrs Fluffy?' Tom's eyes slid towards the black and white cat licking her paws clean on the doorstep. 'What's she done?'

'She keeps chasing the birds. And if she carries on, the Blue-footed Twitterer won't come back to my garden.'

'Well, she can't help it, y'know. She *is* a cat, and cats chase...' Old Tom paused. 'Sorry, what did you say?'

'I said – she keeps chasing the birds.' Roger's eyes shot daggers in Mrs Fluffy's direction. She ignored him completely and moved on to cleaning her whiskers.

'No, the other bit...' Tom struggled to remember the exact words. 'Blue-footed –?'

'Twitterer.'

'I've never 'eard of that one before.' Old Tom scratched his head. 'A blue tit maybe, but not a blue-footed–'

'Twitterer. It's a brand new species. And it appears to have made its home in *my* garden.' Rodger's chest swelled with pride. 'I took the liberty of naming it myself, after its most distinctive feature. *Rogerus pede hyacintho*. Has rather a ring to it, don't you think? I've informed the Ornithological Society, they're very excited.' Suddenly, Rodger's eyes narrowed and he jabbed his finger into Old Tom's chest. 'So just you make sure that cat keeps out of my garden. Especially next Friday.'

Tom stepped out of reach of the finger. 'What's so special about Friday?'

'The Society is sending someone to see the Twitterers for themselves. I don't want the birds to have disappeared before they come.' With a sniff and a final shake of his fist in Mrs Fluffy's direction, Rodger spun on his heel and stormed back home.

Old Tom stood by his garden gate, deep in thought, until the twitcher was out of sight. 'Blue-footed Twitterer?' he murmured. 'I should like to see that one for meself.'

He shuffled inside the house and made a beeline for the bureau in the corner of his lounge. He scrabbled round in the drawers where he kept all sorts of useful stuff, pulling out all the things he didn't want: string, paper, peppermints, pruning shears, emergency sugar lump supply...

'Ah, here we are.' Tom pulled a small tube out of the depths of the bureau. He blew the dust off and gently twisted one end of it; the tube grew to three times its original length. 'Great-great-grandfather's telescope. Knew it'd come in handy one day,' Tom told Mrs Fluffy, who was patting a piece of string in the mistaken belief it was a mouse's tail.

39

Pocketing the telescope, Tom then made a flask of tea, some ham sandwiches, and a twist of paper containing half a dozen peppermints. There was only one more thing he needed. From his bookshelf, Old Tom took down a small, thick volume. Its spine was cracked with age, its pages tea-stained and worn at the edges.

'Crimble's Book of Birds' the title said, in faded gold letters.

*

In the woods behind Rodger's house, Tom found a fallen branch to act as a seat. He settled down to wait, munching happily on a sandwich and occasionally lifting the telescope to his eye so he could squint at Rodger's garden. He stopped chewing when a small brown bird with bright blue legs landed on the bird-table.

'Well, blow me sideways,' Tom muttered.

When another, and then another fluttered down to join the first, Tom completely forgot about his sandwich. Eventually there were a good dozen or so of the little feathered friends contentedly pecking at the seeds Rodger had left out for their lunch.

'Hmmm.' Tom drew the book from his pocket. Thumbing through it, he paused at one particular page. He studied it carefully, chewing his lip while he concentrated. Then he looked again through the telescope at the little brown birds with the bright blue legs. That particular shade of blue reminded Tom of something – but what?

It came to him in a flash. Of course!

When he slammed the book shut, every single Blue-footed Twitterer rose into the air, startled.

'Blue-footed Twitterer indeed. Huh!'

This wasn't a new species. But now he knew what it *was*, Old Tom thought he'd better put things right…

*

All the way to Granny Rainbow's cottage, Tom huffed and puffed.

He didn't stop to admire her garden like normal. He didn't even pause to stroke her cat, Marmaduke. He shuffled as fast as he could to the open front door and raised his fist to knock.

'Stop!'

Tom's hand hovered in mid-air, just an inch away from the pristine paintwork.

Granny Rainbow hurried out of her workshop. 'You look like a man on a mission, Tom,' she said, peering at him over her half moon spectacles.

Old Tom remembered his fist, still poised as though to knock. He shoved it into a pocket and then, to Granny's surprise, he sniffed the door.

'I'm that alright,' he told her. 'We've got a problem.'

'I'd best put the kettle on then. Nothing like a cup of tea to sort a problem.'

Two mugs of tea and six sugar lumps later, Tom finally broached the reason for his visit. 'Now then,' he began, 'you know young Rodger, the twitcher?'

The corners of Granny's mouth twitched in response; young Rodger was seventy if he was a day. She nodded and managed to keep her face straight.

'Well, 'e thinks 'e's discovered a new species of bird. He's calling it the Blue-footed Twitterer.'

'The what?' Granny's eyebrows shot into her fringe.

'You heard.' Tom scowled. 'Now, I may not be a bird hexpert like Roger, but I knows a sparrow when I sees one. Except the ones I saw in his garden 'ave got blue feet. Blue feet the colour of that there door.'

'Oh dear,' said Granny, her eyes following the direction of Tom's pointing finger.

'Now, Rodger has asked a load of nobs from the orni... awnith... ownithol... birdwatching society to come and see this new species tomorrow, and I think 'e's going to make a right fool of hisself 'cos I'm telling you, they are just sparrows with blue feet. We need to get rid of 'em.'

'Yes. Yes, of course. Wait here.' Granny rose and hurried into her workshop. Two minutes later, she returned with a small bottle containing a lovely coral-coloured powder. 'This should do the trick. Mix it all into the water in Rodger's birdbath, and the blue should wash off.'

'I 'ope so,' Tom sighed. 'It'll be one of life's little mysteries, when all the Blue-footed Twitterers disappear overnight.'

'You don't think he'll blame Marmaduke or Mrs Fluffy, do you?' Granny Rainbow looked thoroughly ashamed of herself as she tickled Marmaduke under the chin.

'I don't reckon so,' Old Tom said. 'I'll have to

explain what's happened to Rodger, just so 'e'll let me put this in the water. But...' He glanced sideways at Granny, a slow smile creeping onto his face, '...the next time you paint your front door, don't leave the paint tray out for the birds to walk through.'

Granny Rainbow and Sunflower Saturday

It all started with the sunflower growing competition.

None of the villagers knew quite *when* the village fair had been christened 'Sunflower Saturday'. But everyone knew *why;* over the years, the number of entries to the tallest sunflower competition had grown as fast as the plants themselves. It was not unusual for every family to grow a dozen or more of the giant flowers in the hope that they'd win the coveted trophy.

Old Tom was no different. He'd always choose the sunniest spot in the garden and feed the soil with manure and his special organic growing juice. Then, he'd carefully plant the black-and-white striped seeds, keep his fingers crossed (which didn't make gardening very easy) and hope his sunflowers would grow the tallest.

This year, things weren't looking good.

'Oh deary me, Mrs Fluffy,' Tom said to the cat sitting beside his feet. 'This time last year, they'd almost touched the bedroom window. D'you remember?' He stood a while longer beside the flowerless plants that had only grown as high as his kitchen windowsill, and sighed. 'What are we goin' to do if we don't have sunflowers for Sunflower Saturday?'

Mrs Fluffy only miaowed. Shaking his head, Tom went inside and put the kettle on, pondering the unwelcome thought of Sunflower Saturday without sunflowers while he made the tea.

'I reckon if mine ain't growing, then the Colonel's won't be either,' Tom said, as he stirred the customary three lumps of sugar into his tea. Mrs Fluffy didn't answer; she'd fallen asleep in a patch of sun on the windowsill. Tom didn't mind. He just gazed out of the window and carried on talking to himself. 'I might just wander down to see him. It would be neighbourly, wouldn't it?'

When the tea had been slurped, the biscuits munched and their crumbs brushed under the carpet, Old Tom grabbed his stick and shuffled down to the village, keeping an eye out for sunflowers.

All he saw were stunted plants, none of them taller than waist height. Tom found himself hoping desperately that the Colonel had had better luck with his. The Colonel had a bit of a reputation; there was a field behind his Manor House and every year it was filled with hundreds, if not thousands, of sunflowers. The tallest half-dozen he always kept aside for the competition but the rest he sent down to the village to allow all the houses to be decorated.

This year, Tom wondered whether there would be any spares at all.

Reaching the Manor at last, he crunched up the gravel drive, climbed the steps to the front door and tugged at the bell rope.

Clang! Clang!

The Colonel's butler opened the door. 'Yeees?' he said, looking down his nose at Tom.

'Hullo, Wilson. Is the Colonel in?'

'He's in the field, sir.'

'Righto. I'll wander round.' Tom shuffled off into the garden.

Now, whereas Tom's garden was a higgledy-piggledy mess of flowers of all kinds and colours, growing just where they wanted, the Colonel's was as regimented as the old soldier himself. The plants were in lines so straight they must have been drawn with a ruler, and Tom suspected that the Colonel probably marched along the rows every morning to inspect them. Woe betide a plant that didn't come up to scratch in this garden!

Beyond the garden fence was the field - and the Colonel, leaning on a gate. As Tom approached, the old soldier sighed.

'I don't bally well know what we'll do, Tom, what?' Colonel Green pursed his lips, making his impressive moustache jiggle. 'They'll not be ready in time.'

Old Tom gazed out over the field. It was full of sunflowers – or should have been. Instead, there were hundreds of plants with only stalks and leaves, not a single flower bud in sight.

'I reckon we'll have some sun soon,' Tom said. 'It can't stay grey and cold for ever. And there's a few weeks to go yet.'

'I'm not so sure, what? The coldest spring on record to delay planting, and no sign of a bally summer to bring them on.' The Colonel shook his head. 'We'll just have to have Sunflower Saturday without the sunflowers.'

Tom frowned. He really didn't like the sound of that at all.

*

By the day before the fair, the sunflowers had grown, but no records would be broken this year. The tallest was still only around seven feet tall, when a whopping 15-footer had won last summer. Most disappointing of all, the flower buds remained tightly shut.

The Colonel was getting desperate. He marched up and down the rows of plants in his field, moustache bristling with indignation.

'Now look here! It's just not good enough, chaps. We need you to be open for the big show, don't you know, and you're not playing ball. I reckon you need to get a bally move on and get those petals out, what ho!'

Not a single petal unfurled in response.

With a grunt of disgust, the Colonel headed off to Tom's for a change of scene and a cup of tea.

Down in the village, preparations were well under way for the fair; multi-coloured bunting flapped between the eaves of the houses and the village green was a hive of activity. The rubber ducks were safely corralled on the duckpond, ready for hook-a-duck. Hopefully, this year Arnie Thunk wouldn't try to hook any real ones. The stocks were being tested by the butcher's son in advance of giving the headteacher a soaking; the butcher was currently locked in them and his son was refusing to let him out until he promised sausages and chips for tea. The 'Bowl in One' golf game toilet had been scrubbed and placed under a tree, and the drainpipe for 'Splat the Rat' was under another. The last of the marquee's tent pegs were getting a good bashing from several sweaty men and there were tables and chairs being set up inside, ready for the mountains of cake and gallons of tea that would be served. Would Granny Rainbow's wonderful marmalade and Mother Harberd's super strawberry jam be on sale again, the Colonel wondered. He did so enjoy the one on toast and the other on crumpets...

Sadly, there wasn't a single sunflower.

By the time he'd marched all the way to Old Tom's cottage, the Colonel was in a black mood.

'No sunflowers,' he grumbled at Tom. 'No sunflowers for Sunflower Saturday. Poot!'

Old Tom nodded. 'I know. I've been wondering whether Granny Rainbow might be able to 'elp. What d'you reckon? Shall we go and see her?'

'Well, unless she's got a magic wand, I don't see how she'll bally well manage to do what some of the best gardeners in the village haven't, what!'

'She hasn't got a magic wand,' Tom muttered under his breath. 'But she does make a mean potion.'

When the two men arrived at Granny's cottage, they couldn't believe their eyes. The garden was full of flowers in spite of the weather, and over in the corner, standing taller than either of them were –

'Sunflowers!'

There could be no mistaking the brown faces and yellow petals atop the thick green stalks.

'Hello, Tom, Colonel. What brings you up here, the day before Sunflower Saturday?' Granny Rainbow's smile was as cheerful as the sunflowers.

'Sunflowers,' the Colonel croaked.

'Actually, we 'ave a problem,' Tom added when it became obvious that the Colonel was incapable of saying anything else. 'We 'aven't got any sunflowers, see? They've not opened in time. So it'll be plain old Saturday tomorrow if we can't do something about it. What we think they need is a bit of sunshine.'

'A bit of…oh, I see.' Granny winked at Tom. 'I might have some of that. Give me half a minute.'

The Colonel lowered himself onto Granny's garden seat, unable to tear his eyes away from the corner of the garden. 'Sunflowers,' he murmured every now and again.

Tom patted him on the back. 'There, there, old chap. Granny'll sort us out, don't you worry.'

'Here we are.' Granny reappeared with a glass bottle in her hand, containing a sparkling pale yellow powder so fine it hung in the air like glitter. 'This is my sunshine powder. I think it might be just what you need to get those flowers out.'

The Colonel looked up. 'Sunshine powder? Really?'

'Really. If you want the sunflowers to open, you must sprinkle just a little of this powder on the buds.'

The Colonel rose to his feet. 'Will there be enough?'

'I hope so, because it's all I've got left.' Just for a moment, Granny looked a little sad. Then she brightened. 'Until the sun comes out, anyway. Then I'll make some more. It sounds like the village needs this more than me at the moment.'

'My sunflowers…' There was a glint in the Colonel's eye when he stuck his hand out, but Granny held the bottle just out of reach.

'Ah-ah-aah! You must promise one thing. That you will use this powder on every single sunflower in the village. Not one is to be missed.'

The Colonel began to splutter. 'But…how'm I going to bally well manage that? There could be hundreds of the bally things.'

'If you want a proper Sunflower Saturday, you must promise.' Granny's expression became stern. 'I shan't let you have the powder otherwise.'

'I'll give you a hand,' Tom offered.

'There you are.' Granny beamed. 'With Tom helping, I'm sure you'll find all of them, because I know he likes to keep tabs on any competition he might have. Off you pop! The sooner you start, the sooner you'll finish.'

When they returned to the village, Old Tom and the Colonel began knocking on doors. At every house, they asked the same question.

'Are you growing sunflowers?'

Whenever someone said yes, the Colonel harrumphed. 'I've bought them some bally sunshine, what!' he told the bemused householder.

Then Tom would hold the stepladder while the Colonel climbed up to sprinkle a pinch of the powder – no more, no less – on every bud.

'How do I know you're not sabotaging them? I reckon I stand a good chance of winning this year, got one nearly eight feet high,' Arnie Thunk said, when the Colonel called at his house.

The Colonel snapped to attention. 'Colonel Arthurio Green is an honourable soldier, you rascal,' he roared. 'How dare you suggest otherwise. What!'

By the end of the day, the only sunflowers in need of sunshine powder were those in the Colonel's field.

'I don't know if there's enough in here for this lot,' Old Tom said, squinting at the little bit of yellow still sparkling at the bottom of the bottle.

'Well, we'll do the ones we can.' The Colonel twisted the lid of the bottle off, just as a mischievous breeze whipped the remaining powder into the air.

'That's that then,' Old Tom said, as they watched the powder twinkling and dancing above the plants. 'Let's hope some of that ends up on your flowers.'

The Colonel's shoulders and moustache drooped with disappointment.

*

The next morning, when he opened his bedroom curtains, a blaze of yellow caught the Colonel's eye.

'Well, bless my whiskers,' he said.

When the Colonel marched down to the village later that day, his chest puffed out with pride and a couple of his tallest specimens slung over his shoulder like a rifle, the fair was in full swing. Everywhere he looked, he could see brilliant yellow. Not one bud had stayed shut; every single flower had apparently opened overnight, thanks to Granny's sunshine powder. They filled vases in windows, buckets by front doors and had even been pinned to garden gates. Never had there been such a sunflowery Sunflower Saturday!

The Colonel had just dropped off his competition entries – it looked as though Arnie Thunk's were an inch or so taller – when someone called him.

'Colonel! Over here!'

Granny Rainbow was waving at him from behind a stack of marmalade-filled jars in the refreshment tent, so he wandered over.

'The village is looking lovely, don't you think?' Granny's eyes twinkled behind the lenses of her specs as she lowered her voice. 'I'm so glad you managed to find all the sunflowers.'

'So'm I. Can't have Sunflower Saturday without sunflowers. And thank goodness the sun's finally appeared today too, what!'

Granny nodded. 'I'm already making more sunshine powder, so we'll have enough for next year if we need it.'

The Colonel snorted. 'If we do – it won't be me doing the sprinkling!'

Granny Rainbow and the Little Green Man

It all started with a shooting star.

Granny Rainbow was just closing the bedroom curtains when she saw it. 'Look, Marmaduke! Did you see it? Make a wish, quick!'

Smiling at herself for being so fanciful, but making a wish all the same, Granny pulled the curtains shut, took off her glasses and set them down on the bedside table. Then she kicked off her pink fluffy slippers and slid under the duvet.

'Night-night, Marmaduke,' she said, as the cat settled at her feet. Out winked the light.

The shooting star didn't wink out. It grew bigger and brighter, until finally it crashed into Granny's garden, ploughing up her rhubarb and coming to a halt in the blackberry bramble near the hedge...

*

By lunchtime the next day, Granny Rainbow was rather cross with herself.

'I don't know what's wrong with me, Marmaduke! I'm sure I put the lemonade back in the cupboard yesterday, but it's definitely not there now. And it's not the first thing that's gone missing today, either.' She sighed and a frown clouded her normally cheerful face. 'I must be getting old if my memory's going.'

Marmaduke miaowed.

'A thief? It would have to be a very strange thief, don't you think? So far, there's the bottle of lemonade, half a pot of marmalade and my last few liquorice allsorts gone missing.' She sighed. 'Never mind. I'll make a cup of tea instead, and after lunch I'll spend a couple of hours in the garden. Hopefully the fresh air will clear my head.'

Granny hummed as she weeded the garden, stopping every now and again to laugh at Marmaduke's failed attempts to catch the butterflies and bees which were fluttering and buzzing among the flowers.

'You'll not catch them, you daft cat. Not unless you grow a pair of wings as well,' she told him.

Quite suddenly, Marmaduke dropped to the floor, his rear end wriggling. Then he pounced into the flowers. There was a squeal of surprise and Granny shot to her feet.

'Marmaduke! What have you got? Leave it alone this instant!'

Slinking out of the flowers came a growling Marmaduke, with something clamped very firmly in his mouth.

Granny grabbed him by the scruff of the neck. 'Drop it. Now!' she ordered.

'Miaow!' The cat opened his mouth to protest, and something green dropped from his jaws and scurried back into the flowers.

'Oh! That wasn't a frog,' Granny whispered. Swiftly, she picked Marmaduke up and shut him inside the cottage to keep him out of the way. Then she walked slowly towards the flower bed where the creature had taken refuge. She could see the lupins trembling slightly, even though there was no wind.

'Hello?' she called softly.

The lupins fell still, as though the creature was listening.

'Don't be scared. The cat's inside. There's only me...'

The lupins trembled again and Granny saw two big eyes peering at her from between the leaves. She smiled and held out her hand.

'I won't hurt you...come on out, that's it...oh my!'

61

It definitely wasn't a frog that crept out of the lupins.

It was a little man, no taller than a garden gnome, with bright green skin. He only had three long fingers on each of his hands, his feet were enormous, and there were antennae sticking out of the top of his head.

'Blurble cribble wolk?' he said.

'Pardon?'

Strapped to the creature's arm was a box. He twiddled the knob on the top of it and tried again. 'Speakle creakle eekle?'

Granny shook her head. 'I can't understand that either.'

The creature fiddled with the box again. 'Is this Earth?'

Granny beamed. 'Yes! Yes, it is.'

'I made it! Hooba-dooba! I passed my flying test!' The little man cheered and ran round Granny three times.

'Stop, please! You're making me dizzy!' Granny laughed, trying to watch the peculiar creature.

'But I can't get back!' he gasped, screeching to a halt. 'No-one will know I've passed if I can't get home! Have you got any frekk-ban-jiggle? Or a mechanybob?'

'Um…I don't think so,' Granny said. 'What are they?'

'What I need to fix my spaceship!' The little green man plonked himself down onto the grass and began to cry.

Granny Rainbow couldn't bear to see anyone

upset. 'Oh dear,' and 'there, there,' she murmured over the sound of sobbing. 'Why don't you come into my cottage? Tell me all about it. You never know, I might be able to help.'

*

When Old Tom knocked on the blue front door later that day, it was a very flustered Granny Rainbow who opened it. She had a smudge of green powder on her nose, speckles of blue powder on her dress and red powder underneath her fingernails. Her hair was all blown about and her glasses were askew.

'Tom, am I glad to see you!'

Before he could ask what was wrong, Tom was pulled into Granny's workshop.

'I've tried all the blues and reds and most of the greens,' Granny said, 'but we've yet to work through yellows and oranges. Albi doesn't think purple will be any good at all. You know, I don't know what he'll do if we can't find the frekk-ban-jiggle.'

'The what?' Tom backed away from the strange glint in Granny's green eyes.

'Frekk-ban-jiggle. At least, that's what it sounds like when Albi says it.'

Tom scratched his head. 'And who,' he said slowly, 'is Albi?'

'Of course, how foolish of me. I've not introduced you yet! Albi! Albi? Where are you?'

There was a clinking noise from high up on the shelves. When Tom looked up, he could have sworn there was a green bottle on the pink shelf. Maybe Granny was going a bit doo-lally, mixing up her colours as well as talking rubbish.

'Albi? There's no need to be frightened. It's only Tom. He's a friend.'

What Tom had thought was a green bottle moved. He spluttered and grabbed his chest, pointing at the little green man who'd just crept from behind a pink powder bottle. Tom's mouth opened and closed like a goldfish, but not a single word came out.

Granny nudged him. 'Tom! Don't you know it's rude to stare? This is Albi, from HetzaPretza 26. He's here because his spaceship crashed when it ran out of fuel. Albi, this is Tom. He might look fierce, but he's an old softy really. Now then,' Granny continued, as though it was the most natural thing in the world to be introducing her friend to a little green man. 'Why don't

I make us all a nice cup of tea, and we'll go through the yellows next?'

When Granny came out of the kitchen with a loaded tray, she found Tom and Marmaduke staring at Albi across the dining room table.

'Shoo, Marmaduke. You musn't chase my guest again! This is tea, Albi,' Granny explained, as she poured some into a mug and added milk. 'We drink it all the time on Earth. It's very good for problem-solving. Careful, it's hot.'

Albi peered at the brown liquid and sniffed. His nose wrinkled and he pushed the mug away.

'Granny!' Tom said in a loud whisper. 'Granny – he's an alien!'

'Of course he is.' Granny rolled her eyes. 'Albi's got to mend his spaceship. He needs a mechanybob – which we've worked out is a spanner – and now we need to find the right fuel to get him home again. Unfortunately, Albi's translatabox can't tell us what that is. One lump or two?' She held up the tongs and the bowl of sugar lumps.

'Three please.'

'Frekk-ban-jiggle,' Albi whispered.

66

'Yes, Albi, I know that's what you need. So you see, Tom, I wondered if any of my powders might be the fuel–'

'Frekk-ban-jiggle!' Albi leapt onto the table and snatched the sugar bowl from Granny's hands.

'Here! What you doin'?' Tom spluttered, reaching out to snatch it back.

'It's frekk-ban-jiggle!' Albi said, holding the sugar bowl even closer to his chest.

'Sugar? Sugar's your fuel?' Granny slapped her forehead. 'Of course! What a numpty I am! I bet it was you who made those things disappear – the lemonade, the marmalade and the liquorice allsorts! They've all got sugar in them!'

'But not enough.' Albi's eyes grew wide as he stared at the white cubes. 'This…this is pure frekk-ban-jiggle.'

'Right.' Granny straightened her glasses and took a deep breath. 'How much frekk-ban-jiggle do you need?'

'Lots.'

Tom's head had been flicking from Granny to Albi and back again, almost as though he were watching a tennis match. They finished on Granny.

Her green eyes were twinkling. She marched straight into the kitchen and when she came back, there were two boxes of sugar lumps in her hand.

'Don't give him all of it,' Tom protested. 'What about my tea?'

'I'm sure tea without sugar doesn't taste that bad,' Granny scolded. 'Think of what we're doing for interstellar relationships. Come on, let's sort this spaceship out!'

'Humph.' Tom took a big slurp of tea and pulled a face. He definitely preferred it with sugar.

The spaceship was firmly wedged in the brambles. Tom gave it a hefty tug.

'Ow! Yowch! Ooyah!'

Old Tom got the worst end of the deal; when the spaceship finally came free, the strange machine looked none the worse for its encounter with the bramble bush. Tom, on the other hand, was left bleeding.

He carried the spaceship to the lawn and plonked it down in the middle of the grass. The silvery saucer on legs had what looked like an upturned glass bowl on the top of it and an exhaust funnel underneath.

There were a few dents in the metal and some new scratches and blackberry juice stains, but otherwise it looked none the worse for its adventures.

Granny and Tom looked on as Albi climbed into the glass bowl cockpit with a screwdriver.

'All done,' he announced, moments later. 'The starmeter is working again. Now for the fuel.' He flipped a switch.

A small square hatch opened on the side of the saucer, exactly the right size for a sugar cube. Ten minutes later, Albi declared they had loaded enough frekk-ban-jiggle for him to fly all the way home to HetzaPretza 26.

Granny insisted that he piled the remaining cubes into the cockpit. 'In case of emergencies,' she said.

Albi grinned. 'Thank you, Granny Rainbow. I shall make sure that all translataboxes contain the word 'shu-gaarr' for future flying tests. Just in case... Well, I suppose I really must get going. Back home, they'll be wondering where I've got to. Just wait till they hear what happened!'

'It was very nice to meet you,' Granny said. 'Wasn't it, Tom?'

'Eh? Wassat? Yes, yes, not every day you meet a real-life alien.' Tom nodded and lowered his voice. 'Especially not one who steals the sugar from your tea…oof!'

Granny removed her elbow from Tom's ribs and smiled sweetly.

'Stand back,' Albi called. 'Goodbye!' He twirled the knob on the translatabox. 'Burble crerbly neddly!'

Sparks shot out of the base of the saucer as Albi closed the glass dome. A green flame burned fiercely from the exhaust. Albi gave a wave and with a whoosh, the saucer shot him up into the sky.

Granny and Tom waved until the silver dot with its green flame winked out of sight.

'Sugar lumps in space. What a waste.' Tom's head sank into his shoulders.

Granny squeezed his arm gently. 'Would you like a nice cup of tea?'

'Not without sugar I don't,' Tom grumbled as they walked back into the kitchen.

'Oh, I think I might have a few spare sugar cubes stashed away in the pantry,' Granny told him.

'You put the kettle on and I'll find them, shall I?'

Old Tom straightened his shoulders and grinned. 'That'd be grand!'

Granny Rainbow and the Marmalade Machine

It all started when Old Tom delivered six jars of marmalade to Professor Funkelburger.

Tom liked visiting the Professor's house – you never knew quite what you were going to find when you got there. Last time he visited, the Professor had tried to demonstrate his automatic sheep shearing machine, but all he'd succeeded in doing was giving the sheep some rather unfashionable stripes. The time before that, he'd had some hare-brained scheme for a robotic lawn-mower, which had proceeded to chase the two men into the garden shed without cutting a single blade of grass on the way.

Wondering what on earth the Professor might have invented this time, Tom rang the doorbell.

The door opened, revealing a pair of hugely magnified eyes under a shock of white hair. Tom almost dropped the jars of marmalade.

'Aha! Tom! You have brought marmalade? Gut! Come in…come in. I vos just about to try out my veeding votsit. Come, see!'

Tom's heart settled to a normal rate when he realised it was a pair of safety goggles which had made the Professor look like a giant fly. 'Try out your what?'

'My veeding votsit. You know, to get the veeds out of the ground so my garden looks better, ja?'

A lightbulb popped in Tom's head. 'Weeding! Oh, right.' Leaving the marmalade in the hall, he followed the Professor into the garden.

In the middle of the lawn was a pile of junk.

'Look – my veeding votsit!' the Professor announced, opening his arms as though to embrace the pile. 'Isn't she beautiful? She vill pull up veeds so schnell, I vill have a veed-free garden in no time.'

'Hmm. Prefer a trowel meself,' Tom muttered, as he walked around the strange contraption. He'd never seen anything quite like it. He was certain he could see a bit of old washing line…a tin can…a garden fork… and a pair of coal tongs in the machine.

'Vatch!' The Professor thumped a blue button and the machine sprang into life with a bang and a cloud of black smoke.

'I flick this so…'

A green switch flicked up.

'…and this one I press…'

A yellow knob lit up.

'…and then I twist…'

A large pink dial was turned three times.

'…and off she goes! Veeds avay!'

The machine rolled towards the nearest flower bed, chugging noisily as it did so. A metallic arm, to which the coal tongs were attached, extended towards the plants. The tongs grasped the stem of a begonia firmly and pulled.

Tom looked down at the dandelion still growing happily beside it.

'Teething troubles,' the Professor announced, looking hopeful.

The weeding machine rolled a little further on and the tongs extended again. This time they grabbed a rose bush and yanked it free of the soil.

'No, no no!'

The Professor began to thump all the buttons, but the machine kept rolling on, ignoring the weeds and plucking flowers out instead. Suddenly it froze, mid-pull, and fell silent.

'Hah!' The Professor hid the wire he'd just torn free behind his back. 'Needs vork.'

'I still prefer a trowel,' Tom sniffed.

'Ja, vell... Danke for bringing the marmalade. You know, I so prefer Granny's marmalade. The rind is alvays thinner than Marta Tarter's, and there is something about the taste that sets my tastebuds tingling. Do you not agree? It's just so…orangey.'

'That'll be her secret ingredient,' Tom said. 'By the way, Granny says make these jars last a bit longer this time if you can. She says you'll have to make it yourself if you want more.' Tom looked at the motionless weeding wotsit and chuckled. 'Per'aps you can build a machine to make it for you.'

A strange light came on behind the goggles.

'A marmalade machine,' the Professor whispered.

*

A week later, Granny Rainbow had an unexpected visitor.

'Guten abend,' Profesor Funkelburger said, trying to smooth his hair down. He thrust a bunch of flowers at Granny. 'Please do accept. They were picked fresh today by my Veeding…by my BouquetBot.'

'Why, thank you Professor,' Granny said,

accepting the bouquet of rather bedraggled blooms. 'Won't you come in?'

'Danke.' The Professor followed her into the kitchen and fiddled with his coat buttons while Granny found a vase for the flowers. 'I vas vondering about marmalade,' he began.

'Professor, I can't possibly make any more!' Granny crossed her arms and looked stern. 'I'm all marmaladed out, especially after Sunflower Saturday!'

'No, no, no!' The Professor shook his head and smiled. 'I have built a machine to make marmalade, and it makes plenty. You vill not need to be making it for me.'

'Really?' Granny's eyes widened.

'Ja. But I have a problem,' Professor Funkelburger continued. 'My machine-made marmalade, it does not taste so good as yours.'

'The oranges are plump and juicy?' Granny asked, peering at him over the top of her glasses.

'The best I can get,' the Professor replied.

'Have you cut the rind thin?'

'The machine is set to ultra fine.'

'And you're boiling it for the right time?'

'Until the setting point is reached.'

'Hmmm…'

'It's just not orangey enough. So…I vos vondering whether there is something else you put into the marmalade? Spices? Another citrus fruit?'

Granny looked at the Professor from the corner of her eye.

'A secret ingredient?' he whispered.

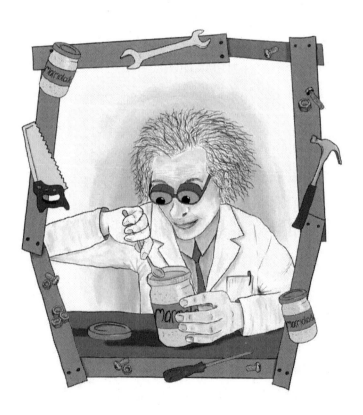

Granny looked thoughtful for a minute or two. 'You're sure the machine is making enough?' she said eventually. 'I won't have to make it for you?'

'Ja.'

'Wait here.' Granny hurried into her workshop. When she returned, she was holding a small bottle, filled with a powder the exact colour of ripe oranges. 'This is what makes my marmalade taste different. Add just a pinch to the mix whenever you make a new batch.'

Granny breathed a huge sigh of relief as she watched the Professor almost run back down the hill.

'Hooray! Now I only have to think about making enough marmalade for myself,' she said.

*

The next morning, she was having second thoughts.

'I'm not sure I should have let him have the powder,' she said to Marmaduke. 'You know what happens if I use too much. Oh, I do hope he's used the right amount.'

All through breakfast, Granny continued to fret.

'It's no good,' she said. 'I've got to go and check he's not done anything daft.'

Before she left home, she weighed out a portion of bright turquoise powder, the same shade as a Mediterranean sea, into a spare bottle.

'Best to be prepared,' she muttered as she slipped it into her pocket.

When she reached the village, she popped into the greengrocers to pick up some oranges for herself. There were plenty of apples and pears and grapes on display, but no oranges.

'Sold out,' the greengrocer told her. 'The Professor bought my entire stock yesterday.'

'Oh dear,' said Granny, and quickened her step. Next, she dropped by the hardware store to get some new preserving jars.

'Sold out,' the shopkeeper said. 'The Professor bought every single one yesterday.'

Granny almost sprinted to the supermarket, but did no more than poke her head in through the door.

'Sugar?' she demanded of the startled girl behind the till.

'Sold out. The Professor–'

'–bought it all yesterday! Oh dear!'

Granny positively flew down the road towards

the Professor's house. She pounded on the front door, but there was no answer, even though she could hear shouting and banging from inside. Alarmed, she ran round the back, where she pulled up in surprise.

A thick river of sticky orangeness was dribbling underneath the back door and oozing down the path.

'Oh my goodness me!'

Granny pushed the back door open. In the middle of the kitchen was the Professor, standing beside a monstrous machine. Both were covered in gloopy blobs of orange marmalade.

The machine was churning out tons of the stuff; it was pouring from a spout like a thick waterfall. Every flat surface was crammed full of jars and it looked as though when the jars had run out, the Professor had used teacups and bowls and anything else he had immediately to hand. At the moment, he was battling with a bucket, full to the brim with the sticky preserve.

'Turn it off!' Granny shouted. 'Turn the machine off!'

'It is off!' the Professor yelled back. 'But it von't stop the marmalade-making!'

'How much of the special ingredient did you add?'

'All of it!'

'What?' Granny gasped. 'I told you just a pinch!'

'But I thought more of it would make it extra orangey!'

'No! Too much just makes it keep expanding!'

'Vot can ve do?' the Professor wailed, reaching for an old metal bathtub.

'Out of the way!' Granny pushed the Professor aside and peered into the huge pan on top of the machine. The marmalade inside was plopping and bubbling, growing in volume even as she watched.

There wasn't a moment to lose. She pulled the little bottle from her pocket and yanked out the cork, dumping its entire contents into the boiling mixture. Granny watched nervously as the turquoise powder was swallowed up by the orange goo.

For a moment or two, nothing happened. But gradually, the bubbling quietened down and the marmalade began to shrink in volume. The waterfall into the bath became a trickle, then a dribble and finally – it stopped. A huge drop of sticky marmalade quivered on the end of the spout for a second before splattering into the tub.

'There, that's done it.'

Professor Funkelburger's wide eyes stared at her over the machine. 'It is finished?'

'Yes.' Granny looked round the kitchen. 'Oh my. You've got an awful lot of marmalade here.'

'But that is good, ja? I like marmalade.' The Professor scooped some from the bathtub and sucked it from his finger. His face twisted into a grimace. 'Yeuch!'

'That's what I was afraid of,' Granny sighed. 'Add too much of the secret ingredient and the orangeyness gets stretched too thin. Horrid, isn't it? Never mind, I'm sure you'll do better on your next batch.'

'Next batch?' The Professor's gaze took in the mess and the hundreds of filled jars and the marmalade machine standing in the middle of it all. 'There von't be a next batch. I have had enough of marmalade. I vill be sticking to Marmite.'

Granny Rainbow and the Big Red Teapot

It all started when Old Tom had the idea for a charity bake-off.

Everyone who wanted to would bake a cake or some biscuits. Then, after Tom had tasted everything – it *was* his idea, so he thought he ought to be the judge – he'd pick a winner. The best baker would receive a bouquet, and all the cake that was left would be sold to raise money for charity.

On the day of the bake-off, the table was positively groaning under the weight of cakes. There was flapjack, millionaire's shortbread, malt cake, scones, honey cake, sultana loaf, strawberry shortcake and many more besides.

Tom didn't know quite where to begin with the judging. The only sensible option seemed to be to start at one end of the table and work his way down, sampling everything on the way.

'These are *so* good,' he said, when he'd finally managed to narrow it down to two entries. In one hand was a slice of Marta Tarter's pear sponge and in the other, a piece of Mother Harberd's apple cake. 'I just can't decide between them. It'll have to be a draw!'

He polished off both slices, wiped the crumbs from his shirt and presented a bunch of his favourite yellow roses to both women. Then he loosened his belt a notch and shuffled home to make himself a cup of tea to wash everything down.

And that's when the trouble began.

The next morning, Marta Tarter turned up on his doorstep with a cake tin.

'I'm so glad you enjoyed my pear sponge yesterday. I've made you something which, I'm sure you'll agree, if you'd tasted this in the bake-off, I'd have won.'

Tom's eyes lit up when he lifted the lid. 'Chocolate truffle sandwich? Why thank you, Marta. I shall enjoy this very much.'

He was in the process of cutting his fifth slice of cake when the doorbell rang again. This time, it was Mother Harberd.

'Oh, Tom,' she said. 'So glad you're in. I was baking again and thought you might like to try my coconut layer cake. It's much tastier than the apple one. I should've made it yesterday, I'm sure it would have scooped first prize.'

'Oh, er, thank you,' Tom said. 'Marta brought a me a cake as well this morning, but I'm sure I'll get through them both by the weekend.'

Mother Harberd's eyes narrowed. 'Oh she did, did she?'

*

The next morning, when Tom wandered out to pick up a newspaper, he was accosted by Marta in the newsagents.

'How did you like the chocolate truffle sandwich, Tom? Told you it was good, didn't I?'

'You did. Though I liked the coconut layer cake too.'

Marta gasped. 'Coconut layer cake?'

Tom wasn't really listening. He'd just caught sight of the headline; 'Baking Bonanza aids Bright Lights Charity' and was feeling rather pleased with himself. 'Yes, Mother Harberd dropped one off. She seemed to think…oh.'

He was talking to thin air.

Strange, Tom thought, as he watched Marta hurrying away.

When he got home, there was a pudding bowl shaped parcel on his doorstep. The note attached to it read:

'Dear Tom, here is my famous syrup sponge, the recipe of which has been handed down through six generations of my family. It's the best you'll ever taste. Enjoy!'

It was signed by Mother Harberd.

'Why are they so keen to feed me cake all of a sudden?' Tom asked Mrs Fluffy.

He'd not long finished his first helping of syrup sponge (with custard) and was contemplating a second helping (with ice cream) when he saw Marta Tarter hurrying up his garden path again.

'Here.' Marta thrust a still-warm loaf tin into his hand. 'Lime and blueberry loaf. Miles better than coconut layer cake.'

'Erm…is it?' Tom scratched his head. 'Does it go with ice cream? Only, I've just got some out of the freezer to try with the syrup sponge.'

'Syrup sponge!' Marta's cheeks turned red. She stamped her foot and almost ran down the garden path.

Old Tom had the distinct feeling that something was going on.

When the doorbell rang at 7am the next morning, Old Tom was still in his pyjamas.

'Not expecting any parcels from the postman,' he muttered, dragging his dressing gown on. 'I'm coming, I'm coming!' he yelled as the doorbell rang again. 'Keep your hair on.'

He opened the door and blinked in surprise at a flour-dusted Marta Tarter and a butter-stained Mother Harberd, who were trying to elbow each other off his doorstep.

'What on earth–?'

'Raspberry roulade!' shouted Marta, shoving a plastic tub under his nose.

'Lemon drizzle cake,' Mother Harberd yelled even louder, attempting to hand over a loaf tin at the same time.

'Ladies, please!' Tom yelped, trying to keep hold of both cakes. 'I've only got one pair of hands!'

The women ignored him and turned to go, jostling each other all the way down the garden path and arguing as they went.

'I believe my sponge will be lighter,' Mother Harberd told Marta Tarter.

'Well, my raspberries are sweeter,' Marta snapped back.

'You do remember I won the gold medal at the Ladies Lunch Club for best baker? You only got silver.'

'Ha! That's because you'd put cranberries in your flapjack, when the recipe clearly stated sultanas.'

'Mrs Bisquit called it creative cooking.'

'I call it cheating!'

'Oh, dear,' said Tom, closing the door quickly to shut out their voices. When he set the latest baked arrivals down on the kitchen table, next to the ones he'd still got to finish, he frowned. 'Oh dear,' he said again. 'I reckon I need to talk to Granny Rainbow.'

Granny wasn't very sympathetic.

'It's your own fault, Tom. You should have picked a clear winner. Those two won't let up now until they know whose cake you think is the best.'

'But I like all cake,' Tom grumbled. 'And those two bake so well, how can I choose? It's like asking me what flowers I prefer, roses or buttercups. They're both yellow, both 'ave their places and look lovely in my garden. But they're very, very different.'

Granny sighed. 'Well, if you can't pick one or the other, we'll have to get Marta and Mother Harberd to realise how silly they're being.'

'Good luck with that,' Tom muttered.

'Oh, I don't think we need luck,' Granny said slowly. 'Just my big red teapot, and maybe a pinch of magic. Here's what we'll do…'

*

Old Tom kept watch at the window.

'Here they come,' he called to Granny. 'And neither of 'em look 'appy.'

'They will,' Granny said, emerging from her workshop. She held up one of her smallest bottles, filled with ruby red powder. 'I have a secret weapon.'

The doorbell rang. Then it rang again.

Granny slipped the bottle into the pocket of her apron, fixed a big smile on her face and flung open the door. 'Ladies! How lovely to see you both! Do come in. Tom, won't you take their coats? Now, do go through to the lounge and make yourselves comfortable.'

Marta took a seat on one end of the sofa, as far away from Mother Harberd as she could manage, clutching an orange-spotted cake tin. The set of her mouth showed quite clearly that she wasn't pleased.

Mother Harberd perched on the edge of a seat at the other end of the room, so stiff that her back never even touched the chair. In her hands was a pink and blue striped cake tin.

'Thank you so much for bringing some of your cake for me to try,' Granny said, apparently unaware that she was holding a conversation all by herself. 'Tom has been telling me how much he's enjoyed your baking, haven't you, Tom?'

'Eh? Oh, yes, yes, lovely cakes,' Tom mumbled as two pairs of eyes swivelled towards him and then back to Granny.

'I've brought a chocolate and cherry gateau,' Marta said, her face stretching into a tight smile. 'I think you'll find it quite the nicest thing you'll have tasted.'

'My orange and spice cake is extraordinarily good. It's a unique recipe,' Mother Harberd chipped in.

The women looked daggers at each other across the room.

Granny took both cake tins and smiled. 'I'll go and put the kettle on, shall I? Do chat among yourselves while I make the tea.'

Marta sniffed and looked out of the window. Mother Harberd stared fixedly at the clock on Granny's mantelpiece.

'Nice weather at the minute, ain't it?' Tom ventured.

Only the clock replied, with a slow steady tick.

When Granny reappeared, Old Tom breathed a

sigh of relief. 'Let me help,' he said, jumping up to take the tray from her. 'They've not said a word to each other,' he whispered. 'It's worse than I thought.'

'Leave it to me.' Granny patted her pocket. She took the lid off the pot – the biggest, reddest teapot that Tom had ever set eyes on – and under the pretence of stirring the leaves, sprinkled the ruby powder into the tea.

Two minutes later, Marta and Mother Harberd were both trying to juggle a cup and saucer *and* a plate of cake.

'I thought you'd like a slice of each others creations,' Granny said with a wink in Tom's direction. 'I'm sure you'll have had quite enough of your own baking and it's always good to try something different.'

'I'm not a big fan of cherries,' Mother Harberd said, putting her plate down on a side table.

'And I can't stand spice,' Marta retorted, setting her plate down on her knee.

Tom added another sugar lump to his mug and stirred. He had a feeling he might need the extra energy.

The ladies sipped their tea. No-one said a word.

Granny kept on smiling, Old Tom kept slurping

his tea, and Marta Tarter and Mother Harberd kept on ignoring each other.

'More tea?' Granny asked when the cups were empty.

Halfway through drinking her second cup, Marta picked up her plate. 'Is it a special blend of spices?' she asked quietly.

Tom looked at her in surprise. 'But you said – ow!' Granny had kicked his ankle under the table and was warning him with a look to stay quiet.

'No, just ordinary mixed spice,' Mother Harberd said, picking up her own plate. 'Do you use black or red cherries?'

'Black. They're sweeter.'

Tom held his breath as both women took a bite of the other's cake. They chewed slowly and swallowed.

'Nice light sponge,' Mother Harberd commented.

'Thank you. The spice isn't overpowering,' Marta replied.

They looked at each other a little sheepishly.

'You make a lovely cake, Marta,' Mother Harberd said.

'So do you.' Marta shook her head. 'Why on earth did we think it was so important to win the bake-off, when we both know how well we can cook?'

Mother Harberd shrugged her shoulders. 'I really don't know. Truce?'

'Truce.'

By the third cup of tea from the big red teapot, the ladies had eaten at least two slices of cake each and were comparing notes on how to make the lightest Victoria sponge. By the fourth, they were swapping recipes.

Tom couldn't believe the change in them both. Granny just sat drinking her tea, a smile playing round the corners of her mouth as she watched her powder working.

They didn't need to pour a fifth cup each. Marta Tarter and Mother Harberd took their leave and walked back down to the village arm-in-arm, chatting and laughing like the friends they once had been.

'You worked miracles there,' Tom said to Granny as they waved goodbye from her doorstep.

'Oh, I don't know. They would have sorted it out eventually. I just speeded things up a bit.'

'I don't think either of 'em will be in a hurry to use me as a judge for their baking in future though.' Tom's stomach suddenly gave a loud rumble.

Granny grinned. 'Probably not. But while there's still some left – would you like another slice of cake?'

Acknowledgements

The danger with saying 'thank you' when you've written and published a book is that you invariably miss someone important out. Suffice to say that this book is not something I've achieved on my own and I could fill *pages* with the friends, family and cloudies who have encouraged and supported me until I felt brave enough to get my stories 'out there'. To every single one of you who's been on the journey so far with me: 'Thank you!'

I do have to say some special thank yous though: to Laura and Imran for their artistic input, to Roo, Stevie, Cat, Sarah, and Luke for 'testing' these stories, and to Debi Alper for being the most wonderful encourager and editor. I'd have given up writing long ago if I'd never met her...

And to all the children I've ever shared a story with: you are my inspiration.

How Granny Rainbow happened...

Early in 2013, I decided to submit a short children's story for a charity collection in aid of the NSPCC.

No sooner had I said 'I'll do it!' when Granny Rainbow jumped into my head, begging to tell me all about the Black Shadow. As a lover of colour – especially rainbows – how could I not write about a colour thief who was defeated by an old lady's cunning and her magic potion?

Then my son told me I had to write more about Granny; 'One story for every colour of the rainbow, please.'

Different things inspired the stories; my dad loves feeding the birds in his garden, my children play the violin and double bass, and Sunflower Saturday owes a lot to the many school fairs I've helped with. I began to wonder about publishing them as a book – an illustrated book.

Laura had already illustrated a children's book before leaving school and I thought maybe she'd like to be involved. Luckily for me, she said 'yes!'

This is the result. I hope you enjoy it.

10 fun facts about Katherine:

1. She used to have a job pickling eggs.
2. She once swam with dolphins in the sea off the coast of New Zealand.
3. She loves all things rainbow – but the colours have to be 'true' and in the right order.
4. She has a cat called Timmy, who bites her when he's hungry and ignores her most of the rest of the time.
5. Her family owns a 55m high wind turbine, called Bob.
6. She has a phobia about piercings, especially on the face.
7. She loves liquorice and cold chicken – just not both at the same time.
8. She loves swimming in the sea in Sardinia.
9. Her favourite flower is lily of the valley, but it won't grow in her garden.
10. She hates being cold and often resorts to a pair of fingerless gloves when typing her stories in the winter months.

Katherine's website: http://microscribbler.wix.com/katherine-hetzel

10 fun facts about Laura :

1. She has always loved drawing and painting.
2. She is left-handed.
3. She loves reading manga and watching anime.
4. She's studying Graphic Design and Illustration at De Montfort University.
5. She hates it when her younger sister jokes about being taller.
6. She loves reading and watching anything to do with fantasy.
7. She has fainted three times in public (very embarrassing!)
8. She has a faint scar on the palm of her left hand where she stabbed herself (accidentally) with a pencil at primary school.
9. Her favourite colour is purple.
10. Her favourite quote is 'Regret looks back. Fear looks around. Worry looks in. Faith looks up.' Nicky Gumbel